The Great White House Breakout

by Helen Thomas & Chip Bok

 Dial Books for Young Readers

"I hope this magical book will open the eyes of young people to the great history of America, and the beauty of Washington"
—Helen Thomas

"For friends of lab rats everywhere"
—Chip Bok

WHITE HOUSE ORDERS: KEEP AN EYE ON SAM

DIAL BOOKS FOR YOUNG READERS • A division of Penguin Young Readers Group • Published by The Penguin Group • Penguin Group (USA) Inc., 375 Hudson Street, New York, NY 10014, U.S.A. • Penguin Group (Canada), 90 Eglinton Avenue East, Suite 700, Toronto, Ontario, Canada M4P 2Y3 (a division of Pearson Penguin Canada Inc.) • Penguin Books Ltd, 80 Strand, London WC2R ORL, England • Penguin Ireland, 25 St. Stephen's Green, Dublin 2, Ireland (a division of Penguin Books Ltd) Penguin Group (Australia), 250 Camberwell Road, Camberwell, Victoria 3124, Australia (a division of Pearson Australia Group Pty Ltd) • Penguin Books India Pvt Ltd, 11 Community Centre, Panchsheel Park, New Delhi – 110 017, India • Penguin Group (NZ), 67 Apollo Drive, Rosedale, North Shore 0632, New Zealand (a division of Pearson New Zealand Ltd) • Penguin Books (South Africa) (Pty) Ltd, 24 Sturdee Avenue, Rosebank, Johannesburg 2196, South Africa • Penguin Books Ltd, Registered Offices: 80 Strand, London WC2R ORL, England

Text copyright © 2008 by Helen Thomas
Pictures copyright © 2008 by Chip Bok

The publisher does not have any control over and does not assume any responsibility for author or third-party websites or their content.
Text set in OpalsHand
Manufactured in China on acid-free paper

10 9 8 7 6 5 4 3 2 1

Library of Congress Cataloging-in-Publication
Data available upon request

I am Sam. My mom and dad work at home.
I have to be careful not to bother them when I play.

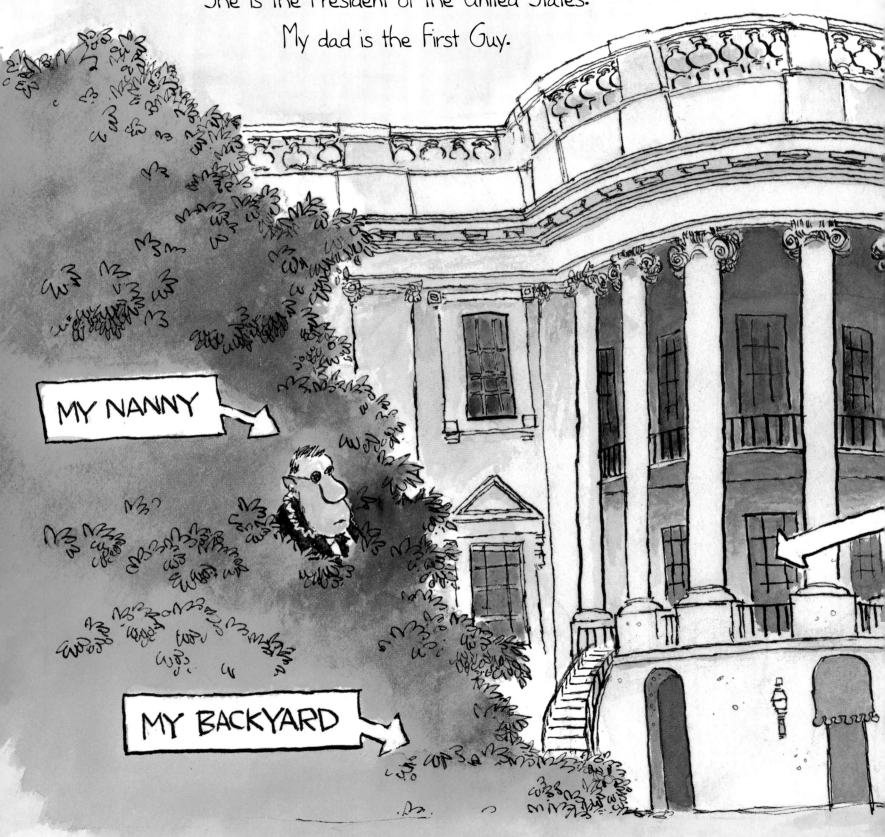

The guys with the phone cords in their ears are always listening to us.
I think my mom hired them to make sure we don't have any fun.

So we just hang out
and bounce around the house,

LINCOLN
BEDROOM

and sometimes we look for my mom in her office. It's an oval, just like a racetrack.

Warren is almost as important as Mom. When he walks into a room, everyone stands. I think it has something to do with Leonard—he's trying out for our swim team.

"If we could get out of here, you'd see Washington isn't such a bad place," Leonard said one day, trying to cheer me up. Before he lived with us, Leonard was a lab rat for NASA, so he's really smart. He laid out a brilliant escape plan in our secret war room. When the guests came for dinner, Leonard would dash through the dining room . . .

(which he did perfectly—Leonard was the life of the party!)

And while everyone was distracted, we'd make our big break. (Victory!)

In the morning, we met undercover rats at the Spy Museum.

Then we crossed the Atlantic.

Later, I found some old papers to read while Leonard researched dinosaurs . . .

and then we looked for pirates.

Soon it was getting dark. And cold. This time, it was a little scary. We curled up on a nice man's lap to sleep.

When we woke up, I could tell Warren wished he had slept in my bed too.
"Leonard?" I asked. "Can we go home? I miss Mom."
"If only we had some altitude, we could see where home is," he sighed.

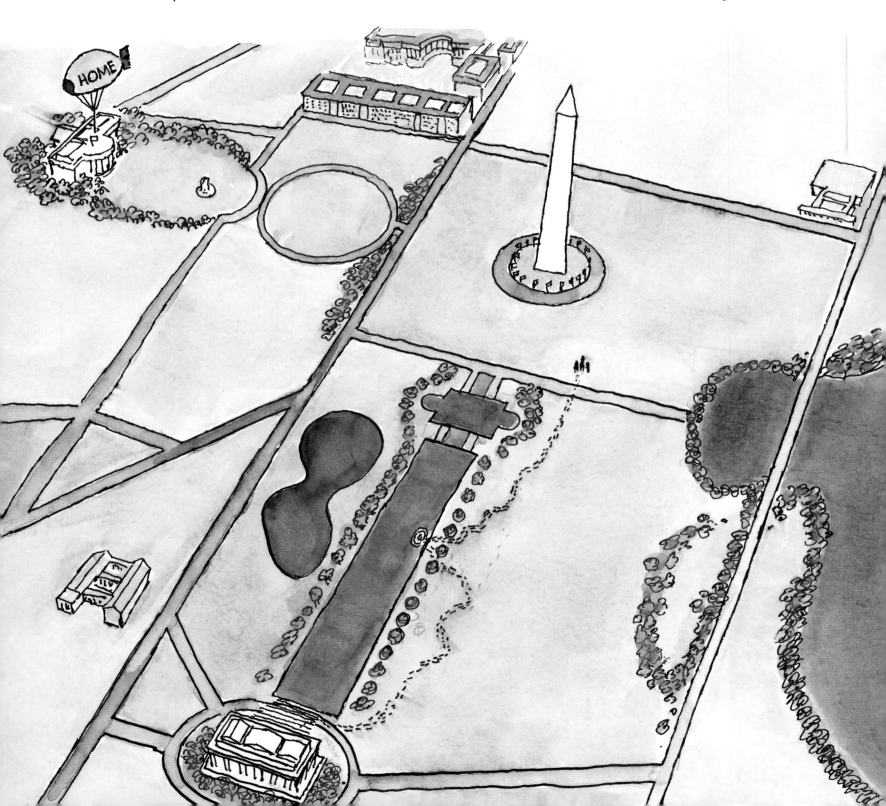

Then Leonard found a broken kite. "Perfect! We'll use this as a spy satellite to find your house. My special space glue should fix it up in no time."

"What's missing now," Leonard announced, "is a tail and a great puff of wind."

WHOOSH

When we got back on the ground, Mom was waiting.
I guess she missed us too.

Mom said the press will have a field day with this.
I wonder what kind of games they'll play. Maybe they'll fly kites!